Acknowledgments

This book is dedicated to my grandchildren, with all my love. May you always love Christmas time and let it take you to a happy place in life, a time when your imagination could flow free with bedtime stories we made up and giggled over.

I want to thank my wonderful loving mother who always encouraged me to pen my stories.

The Adventure of Ben and Walter North Pole Elves

Printed in the United States of America

First Printing, 2018

The Adventure of Ben and Walter North Pole Elves

Written by Leisa Miller Harrison
Illustrated by Leon Hollins III

This is a story about two elves who work for Santa Claus. Their names are Ben and Walter, and they are the inspection elves. They inspect and stamp every toy with Santa's North Pole Seal-of-Approval before it can be magically placed into Santa's toy bag for delivery to a child.

INSPECTION
ELF #246
INSPECTION
ELF #014

One morning, Ben and Walter were taking a break, drinking hot chocolate and eating candy canes. While Ben was stirring his hot chocolate with his candy cane, he peered out the window and saw a great surprise.

Tied to a pole outside was a beautiful, bright-colored hot air balloon gently dancing in the breeze…

Ben ran to find Santa and asked him if he and Walter could take a ride in the beautiful hot air balloon! Santa told him there was no time for play, Christmas was near. Ben was so sad, but he went back to work.

Throughout the day, Ben would glance out at the balloon dreaming of taking it high in the sky and flying with the birds.

That night after work, all the elves went into a very large bedroom shared by every elf. There were rows and rows of tiny beds with elf boots at the end of each bed. Hats were hung on bedpost-ends, with tiny jackets hung on the other end post. Elves sleep in red long pajamas that keep them warm and cozy at night. So, during the night, Ben looked around to make sure all the other elves were sleeping and then tip-toed over in his pajamas to Walter.

Ben whispered in Walter's ear, "Let's go see the beautiful hot air balloon!" Walter agreed, and they carefully put on their tiny clothes and sneaked out like quiet little mice.

Walter
BEN

Before they knew it, they were outside looking up in the air at the most colorful hot air balloon either one of them had ever seen. Ben said to Walter, "Let's get in the basket and pull on the rope to bring the balloon down, then we will let go of the rope and pop up into the air just like we were really flying high in the sky!" Well, Ben and Walter were having a great time pulling on that rope, making the balloon come down to the ground, and then letting the rope go so the balloon would jerk up fast into the air.

They did this over and over and over…down and up…down and up.

It was getting so late, but it appeared Ben could do this all night. Not Walter, though; he told Ben he was very tired and wanted to go back to sleep. Ben begged, "Just one more time, Walter, please?" Walter agreed to do it one more time, but just as Ben let go of the rope, it popped, snapped, and broke!

Santa's
Toy

As the balloon floated up, up, and away, Ben and Walter started shouting for help.

"Santa! Rudolph!" Over and over they cried, but because of the wind and snow no one could hear them!

As the wind carried them away high in the sky, Santa Land got smaller, smaller, and smaller, until they couldn’t see it anymore.

Santa
HELP!

The next morning, all the other elves were busy making toys; but Santa noticed that toys were piling up at the Seal-of-Approval workstation. He looked around and did not see Ben nor Walter. Santa walked over to the Head Elf and asked, "Where are Ben and Walter?" The Head Elf said, "No one has seen them this morning."

Santa went to see if they were in the Stamp Room looking for ink to put on the stamp, but they weren't in the room. So Santa scratched his head in thought, "Where can those two elves be?" Just then he shouted, "Ben! Walter! Hot air balloon!" So he ran to the nearest window...

SANTA'S
TOY

Santa saw the balloon was missing and sounded the emergency alarm. All the workers stopped, and Santa said, "We have an emergency! Ben and Walter must have taken the hot air balloon last night. We must go find them, for they will not last long in this weather. I need you, Rudolph, to get your team ready for a sleigh ride now!" As Santa started to take off, the snow storm was getting very heavy, so he told Rudolph to brighten his nose like never before!

He yelled for all to pray for everyone's safety as he led his sleigh off to find the elves.

Santa and his sleigh flew out and above the snowstorm, high above the Earth, but there was still no sign of Ben and Walter. Santa was getting very worried that the hot air balloon had crashed somewhere. He told his team of reindeer to listen with their keen ears, and he too placed his finger on his nose to up his hearing with a magic touch. Again, Santa asked Rudolph if he could brighten his nose anymore in hopes that Ben and Walter would see it as a beacon to let them know that they were looking for them.

Walter glanced out over the moon looking for any help. Ben was no help at all because all he could do was be mad at himself for not listening to Santa. Then, Walter started shouting, "Ben! Look, we're saved." They started shouting as loud as they could, "Here we are! Up here, up here!"

Santa with his keen hearing looked up and couldn't believe his eyes.

There above the stars, sitting on the crescent moon, were the two elves with the deflated hot air balloon. They were looking down at Santa and his sleigh, so happy to be found.

Santa put them in the sleigh and packed the hot air balloon into his bag. As they landed back in the North Pole, all the elves heard them coming and lined up cheering with joy that Ben and Walter had been found safely.

Ben and Walter were so glad to be back home. As they walked through the crowd, all the other elves started shaking their heads and pointing their tiny fingers at Ben and Walter for what had happened. Ben and Walter had their heads down as they walked through the path of elves. Then, at the end of the path, they saw Mrs. Claus holding two cups of hot chocolate with candy canes sticking out for them, this made them smile with joy.

"Oh! Thank you so very much, Mrs. Claus!" said the elves. Mrs. Claus told them because they had misbehaved and had worried everyone—and not to mention that it's just a few days till Christmas—that this hot chocolate was made special. "What do you mean 'special'?" asked Ben. "Well, you and Walter will go to sleep and have sweet dreams for 100 years before you wake again!"

Don't worry children, 100 elf years may seem a long time to you, but you see elves are very old. Time is different at the North Pole. So the elves were sent to bed in a special room. Above the door a sign read, "Dream Room".

Hot Cocoa

Do you know what Ben and Walter were dreaming of while in the Dream Room? Not hot chocolate, not eating Christmas cookies, not even candy canes. They were dreaming of being Santa Claus… yes, Santa Claus!

If they were Santa, they would be tall and jolly, get to deliver toys to every child, and eat cookies from all over the world. What a cool dream to have. Can you imagine flying in a reindeer-driven sleigh bringing happiness to all the good children in the whole world, plus eating all those yummy cookies all in one night?

dream room

Well, while Ben and Walter were having their amazing dreams, Santa was looking at the pile of toys waiting on Santa's Seal-of-Approval before they could be put into his magic bag of toys. The pile just kept growing, growing, and growing almost to the point it looked like a Christmas tree made of toys.

Remember, it's just a few days till Christmas...

So, Santa knew he had to find some other elves to take over for Ben and Walter, and fast. He walked up to the top floor in the toy factory, so he could see over all the elves. As he looked around at all of the busy elves doing their work, he scratched his head and thought to himself, "How can I spare any of the elves?" As you know, every elf has a very important job and is very busy this close to Christmas.

As Santa stepped around to look over the other side, he almost stepped on the smallest twin girls ever born at the North Pole, Dolly and Holly. Dolly has blond hair and is very sassy, and Holly has red hair and is very spirited. Santa yelled, "Dolly, Holly, I almost flatted you two like Christmas Pancakes."

The girls just giggled. Santa asked, "What can I do for you two? I'm very busy at the moment trying to find replacements for Ben and Walter." Then Santa looked at that pile of toys backed up waiting for approval.

"Well, Santa," Dolly said with her head held up high trying to look all grown up, "Holly and I were wondering, since Ben and Walter are asleep in the Dream Room, can we have their jobs?" "I promise we can do it and get it all done before Christmas Eve." Holly confirmed, "We are ready and will be the fastest and best Santa Seal-of-Approval stampers you have ever seen."

Santa asked the girls, "What about your jobs?" Dolly told Santa all the girl dolls had their hair fixed, dresses pressed, and were boxed and ready for approval, "See, they're in that pile just waiting."

"I see," said Santa as he looked around at the busy elves knowing he had no other choice, but to take Dolly and Holly up on their offer to help.

"Alright, Dolly and Holly, the jobs are yours. Do you think you can do it?" asked Santa.

"Oh yes, Santa! We were born for this job and we won't let you down," said Dolly.

"Ok, then girls, get to work; there's no time for rest!" Santa replied.

And to work they went. They were so happy that Dolly started to sing as loud as she could and Holly started to dance to the tune of a little song:

"Stamp, stamp, stamp
into the sack we will pack,
Dolly and Holly are the best,
While Ben and Walter rest,
Every toy will bring a kid joy,
Stamp, stamp, stamp."

Well, Christmas came and went twice before Ben and Walter woke up from their 100-year elf nap. Santa went into the Dream Room knowing this was the day Ben and Walter would awake from their long winter's nap.

With Santa leaning on the door, Ben and Walter starting to stretch and yawn as they opened their eyes. Santa said, "Well, it's about time you two woke up! Christmas is 9 months away and you two have to get to work."
"Wait, what? Did we sleep through Christmas?" Ben exclaimed.
"Why yes you did—two of them!" said Santa.

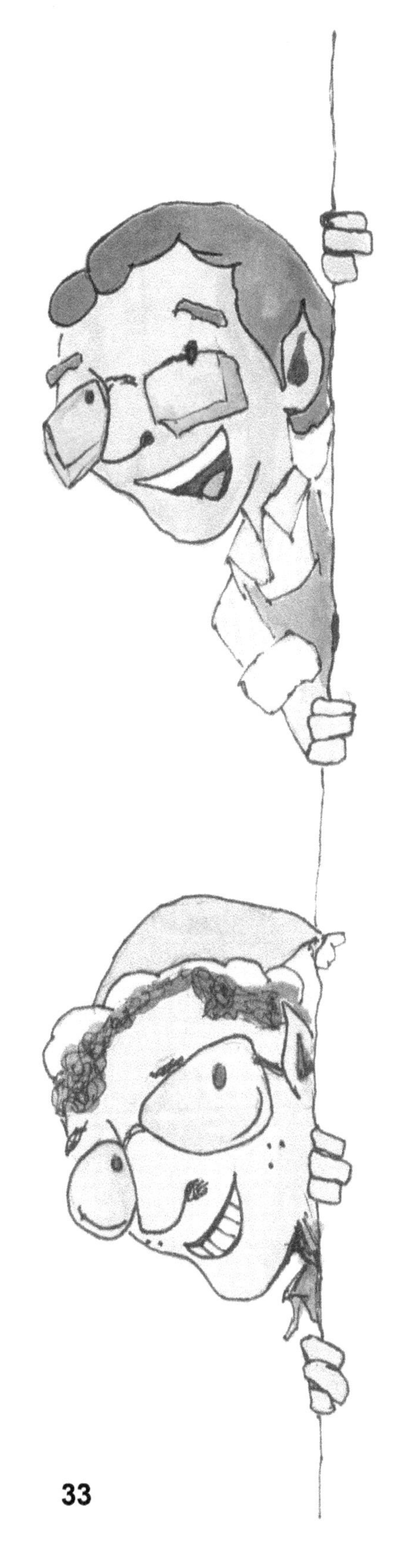

"Oh, no," Walter said, with his head held down. Then, Santa asked them about their dreams. They both started to tell him their dreams, but before they could say a word Santa said, "No, wait. Tell me later, we have no time now. I need you two to get to work so the other elves can move up to new jobs."

"Ok," said Ben and Walter as they started to grab some cookies and milk on the way to the toy workshop. "Oh no," said Santa, "Your jobs are no longer in the toy workshop."

"What!" yelled Ben. "Well, since you two couldn't stay out of trouble, I had to replace you with Dolly and Holly for the past two Christmases, and—to tell you the truth—they are excellent at it and are now *Top Santa Seal Approvers* forever."

"No way," said the two elves glaring at each other in disbelief. "Oh no," said Walter. So he asked, "Well, Santa, what are our new jobs? Are we going to be doing Weather alerts, mail deliveries, or cookie tasting?" "Oh, how we would love that one; all the cookies we want all year round," said Ben, "Yummy!"

"Nope! You two follow me," Santa said as he walked over to the reindeer barn. As they walked in, they said hello to Rudolph, Dasher, Dancer, Prancer, Vixen, Comet, Cupid, Donner, and Blitzen. "Oh," said Ben, "We're going to be taking the sleigh on test flights; we are now Practice Pilots!" "Yippee!" said Ben and Walter with joy, "We will love this job, Santa!"

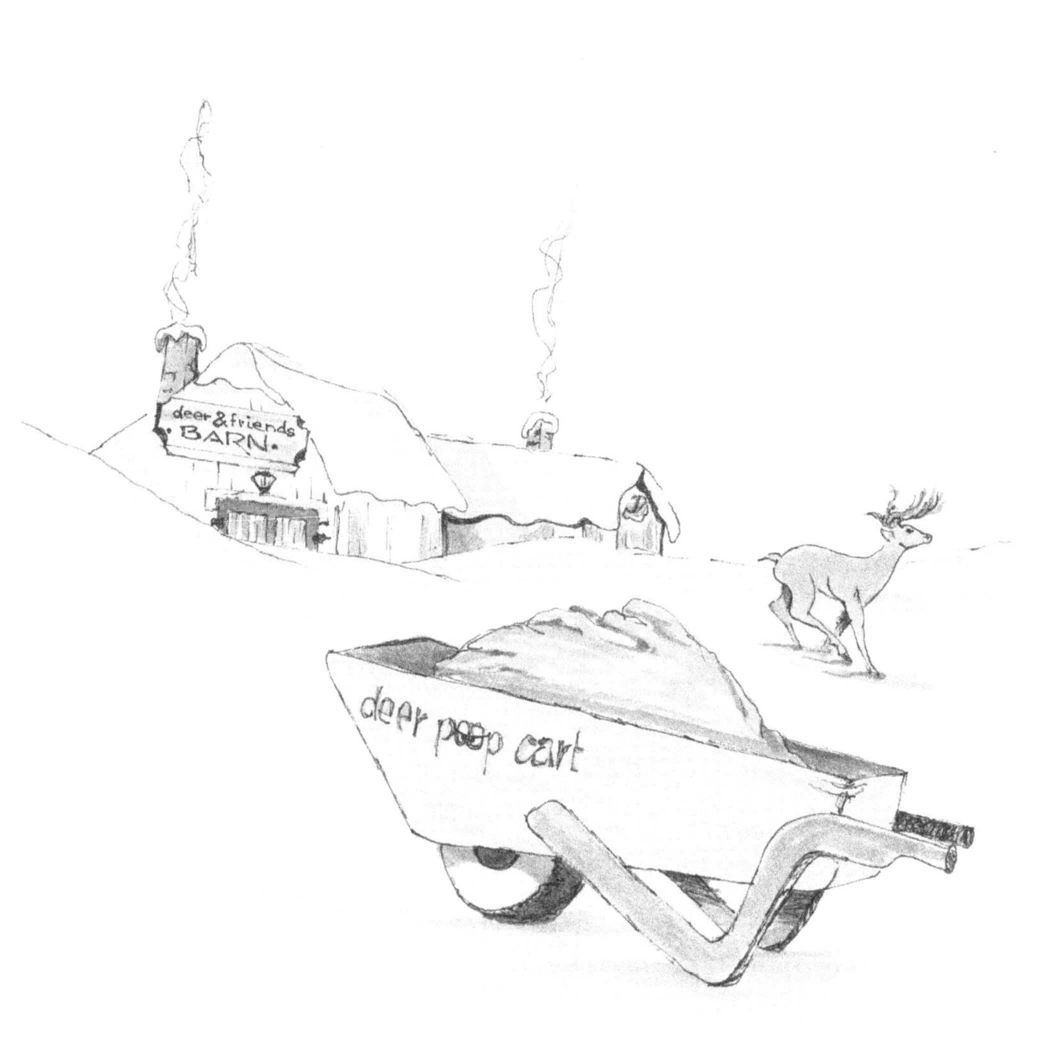
deer & friends
BARN
deer poop cart

"Well," said Santa, "You're NOT going to be pilots; you two are now the new reindeer keepers and are in charge of keeping Rudolph, Dasher, Dancer, Prancer, Vixen, Comet, Cupid, Donner, and Blitzen happy and loved."

"Oh, and don't forget you are also the new Pooper Scoopers for all the animals that live in the barn too!" Ben and Walter looked with their eyes wide open at all the deer, dogs, cats, rabbits, and birds that lived in the barn too. "Now Santa," said Ben, "is this a joke?"

"No joke," said Santa, "I want everyone to know the importance of doing right from wrong, like all the kids in the world; they have to be good or not receive a toy. Now how would that look if I let my elves have special treatment? Then kids would be bad all year and still want toys at Christmas."

Ben and Walter started to fight, blaming each other for losing their jobs as Santa Seal-of-Approval stampers and going all the way down to barn keepers. Most of all, they hated the thought of being Pooper Scoopers too. Not paying attention to the very big pile of reindeer poop, they both pushed each other into it!

"Phew," they yelled. Santa just turned around and walked away shaking his head while laughing, "Ho-ho-ho," at Ben and Walter.

"Ho-Ho-Ho, those two don't need to know it's just till the new hot air balloon building is completed and then they will get to be in charge of it, ho-ho-ho," laughed Santa. "Plus, Dan and Jan love being in charge of the reindeer barn, so I just gave them a trip to the Shoemaker's Store for a short vacation," laughed Santa, "Ho-ho-ho!"

The End

Lightning Source UK Ltd.
Milton Keynes UK
UKHW050749140119
335532UK00008B/101/P